Christmas at Home

101 ADVENT ACTIVITIES FOR KIDS

WRITTEN AND COMPILED BY
ELLYN SANNA

BARBOUR
PUBLISHING, INC.
Uhrichsville, Ohio

© 2000 by Barbour Publishing, Inc.

ISBN 1-57748-942-X

All rights reserved. No part of this publication may be reproduced or transmitted in any form or by any means without written permission of the publisher.

All Scripture quotations, unless otherwise noted, are taken from the King James Version of the Bible.

Scripture quotations marked (NIV) are taken from the HOLY BIBLE, NEW INTERNATIONAL VERSION®. NIV®. Copyright © 1973, 1978, 1984 by International Bible Society. Used by permission of Zondervan Publishing House. All rights reserved.

Scripture quotations marked (NLT) are taken from the *Holy Bible*, NEW LIVING TRANSLATION, copyright © 1996. Used by permission of Tyndale House Publishers, Inc. Wheaton, Illinois 60189, U.S.A. All rights reserved.

Published by Barbour Publishing, Inc., P. O. Box 719, Uhrichsville, OH 44683
http://www.barbourbooks.com

Printed in Canada.

Introduction

What does Advent mean to you? Does it mean a time of the year when you have too much to do in too little time? Does it mean a relentless countdown of shopping days? Does it mean a time of hectic family get-togethers and frantic office parties?

Or does it mean a time when we celebrate the birth of Love into our world?

I ask myself these questions every year as the Advent season begins. I also ask myself another question: What do I want Advent to mean to my children? Children seem to grasp the magic and miracle of Christmas so much better than us tired adults—but they too can be distracted by our world's busyness and rampant materialism.

If you want the kids in your life to celebrate the love you have for one another, if you want them to reach out to others in need, and if, most of all, you want them to focus on the coming of Christ this Advent, then the activities in this book will help your family find the true meaning of Christmas.

You have enough to do at this busy season, so don't feel this book will simply add to the heavy load of responsibilities you carry. You certainly don't have to do *all* of these activities—but you might want to try those you think your family would most enjoy. Take time this year to stop all the hustle and bustle. Take time to enjoy each other.

These activities are designed for kids—but as you participate in them, you may be surprised to find how much fun Advent can be. Christmas calls to the child in all of us, asking us to play, to rejoice, and to wonder. . .as we prepare our hearts and homes for the Christ Child's coming.

Never-Ending Love

At some point during Advent make wreath cookies to symbolize the never-ending love of Jesus. Use rolled sugar cookie dough (when I'm short on time, I buy the kind that comes pre-made); color half of it green, and leave the other half white. Roll out one tablespoon of each color of dough as long and wide as a pencil. Twist the rolls of dough together like a rope, and shape the twist into a wreath. As you bake, and later as you nibble, talk with your children about why a circle symbolizes Christ's love that never ends.

Love never fails.
1 CORINTHIANS 13:8 NIV

Advent Banner

Over the years I've experimented with different types of Advent calendars to use with my children. This one is probably about the simplest.

Cut a 4-foot by 8-inch rectangle of green felt, then sew on it a 4-foot by 3-inch strip of red felt, leaving the top of the red rectangle open. Divide the red strip into segments by sewing a seam through the red and green material every 2 inches, making pockets. Cut numbers from green felt, 1 through 24, and glue them to the red pockets. You may wish to embroider your banner or decorate it with rickrack or other decoration—or you can keep it very simple.

At the beginning of Advent, write Bible verses on small pieces of paper and tuck them into the pockets. Then have your kids begin or end each day of Advent by taking turns reading a Bible verse, followed by a prayer.

Thy word have I hid in mine heart.
PSALM 119:11

A Christmas Chain

A Christmas chain, made with 25 red and green construction paper loops, is a visual way to count down the days till Christmas. Each day a child can tear off a loop of the chain.

Making the chain is also an important part of this activity. (If I cut the strips of red and green paper, I found that even my youngest child could glue or staple them together.) On the green links have the children write things for which they thank God (pets, food, friends, God's Word, water, the seasons, Grandma and Grandpa, books, laughter, etc.). On the red chains write the names of friends and extended family members.

Then use the link each day for a time of family prayer. On green days give thanks to God, and on red days ask His blessing and help for a loved one.

> *Advent is like a chain of blessings,*
> *each one better than the last.*
> *Let us regain the anticipation of childhood,*
> *and welcome this holy season. . . .*
> ALEXANDER PHILLIPS

The Twelve Days of Christmas

Twelve days before Christmas, take a small gift to a family in need (perhaps a neighbor—a new family at church—someone who has a sick family member or a new baby in the house). Secretly set the gift (food, warm gloves, an inexpensive baby item, whatever seems appropriate), decorated with a bow, on the porch. The next night put two small items, each with a bow, at the same spot. The third night take three gifts. Each successive night stealthily deliver your gifts. You'll need creativity to deliver without being discovered! On Christmas Eve take your last gift and sing "The 12 Days of Christmas," putting your items into the song. Children love the secrecy and surprise.

*The Lord Jesus himself said:
"It is more blessed to give than to receive."*

ACTS 20:35 NIV

Fondue Party

Have a chocolate fondue party, either with friends or with just your family. I've noticed in my own family that any time we eat somewhere besides the normal place, my kids find any meal much more fun—so for this special Advent repast, spread an old sheet in the middle of the living room floor, put the fondue pot in the middle, and then have everyone sit cross-legged around the pot.

While you dip bits of fruit, graham crackers, and sugar cookies into the melted chocolate, take turns reading a Christmas story out loud. (*The Best Christmas Pageant Ever* is one favorite with kids—or read some other Christmas story that emphasizes the Christian message.)

Let us not forget to simply enjoy each other this season, O Lord. . . .

ALEXANDER PHILLIPS

Christmas Bread

On Christmas Eve, as a family, make Christmas bread in the shape of a wreath. (Divide the dough into 3 long rolls and braid them, then pinch the ends together.) Eat the bread for your Christmas Eve dinner, reminding your children that Jesus is the Bread of Life.

Jesus said unto them,
I am the bread of life:
he that cometh to me shall never hunger.
JOHN 6:35

Advent Song

Spend some time each day singing Christmas songs together (let the kids take turns picking the song). This is an especially good activity for the car. I know when I'm feeling pressured and irritable, singing a Christmas carol helps me regain my sense of Christmas joy as much as it helps my children.

The LORD is my strength and my song.
PSALM 118:14 NIV

Advent Yule

The Yule log was a way our ancestors once symbolized the burning of the past. Combine this ancient tradition with your Advent activities by going to the woods each year with your children to find a small piece of log to use as a family centerpiece. Drill candle-sized holes in it for the Advent candles. (You may need to level off the bottom so the log will sit flat.)

Then once a week at your evening meal light that week's candles, read an Advent Scripture, and take turns forgiving each other for events from the past. Use this as a time to celebrate your forgiveness of each other as you rejoice in the forgiveness Christ gives us all.

For if ye forgive men their trespasses, your heavenly Father will also forgive you.

MATTHEW 6:14

"Real" Yule

You need a fireplace to carry out the "real Yule" log ritual. Have the kids comb the woods for a large, knotty, hardwood log. If it's water-soaked, all the better, as it will burn slower. Some evening in Advent, make a hot fire with dry kindling and smaller pieces of wood, then top it with the Yule log. As long as the Yule log burns (and you may be able to keep it burning for several days), follow the ancient tradition and ban all nonessential work. Have family members write on slips of paper the things they are sorry for that happened during the past year; they may share these with the rest of the family, or they may choose to keep them private. Then one by one, drop them into the Yule flames to symbolize the freedom in Christ we have from sin. When the log finally burns out, save a piece of it to start next year's Yule log.

Blessed are they whose iniquities are forgiven.

ROMANS 4:7

A Shower for the Baby Jesus

Our church tried an activity this year that you and your kids might like to try as well: Host a baby shower for Baby Jesus. Invite other families, and ask them to bring baby gifts to be donated to a local charity for unwed mothers. Play the usual shower games and celebrate the chance to demonstrate love to a poor Child whose family lacked even a bed in which to lay Him.

Verily I say unto you,
Inasmuch as ye have done it unto one of the least of these...
ye have done it unto me.
MATTHEW 25:40

Here's an invitation you might want to send out for your baby shower:

Christmas is the celebration of a birth, a baby's birth. That baby appeared to be illegitimate, poor, even homeless. That baby was Jesus, who grew to be the Christ, the Savior of the world! This year, we're inviting you to celebrate Christmas by bringing a gift to a baby shower. The baby may be illegitimate, poor, or even homeless. It will be a baby born to someone who is being ministered to by the local pregnancy center. We hope the baby will grow to be someone who will share the good news of Christ, the Savior of the world. Spend as much or as little as you like. Gifts may be new, or as-good-as-new. Come and celebrate a very special Baby's birth.

Making the Baby's Bed

Put the names of all the family members in a bowl, and on each weekend of Advent have each family member draw a name. Place a "manger" under the Christmas tree (if you don't have a crèche manger, a bread pan or a shoe box will work), with a bag of straw beside it. Throughout the week, have both children and adults do kind deeds for the persons whose names they drew, without revealing their identity. For every kind act performed, place a piece of straw in the manger. Each weekend draw a new name so that you spread your kind deeds throughout the family. The aim is to see how full and soft you can make the manger before Christmas Eve. On Christmas day, lay the Christ Child (again, if you don't have a crèche set, use a doll) in the manger.

This activity's fun comes from giving someone else pleasure, helping children to focus more on others than themselves.

Put on. . .kindness.
COLOSSIANS 3:12

St. Nicholas Day

One way to counteract the commercialism of Santa Claus without doing away with him all together is to talk about the historical St. Nicholas, a man who served God by giving to children. Celebrate St. Nicholas Day on December 5 by having children put their shoes outside their doors before they go to bed, and fill them with small gifts for them to find in the morning.

Maybe an even better activity for December 5 is to have your children sort through their toys and games for still-new items they could donate to a local shelter or other charity, so that they too can follow in St. Nicholas's footsteps.

Blessed is he that considereth the poor.

PSALM 41:1

Advent Candle

Catalogs and gift stores offer tall white candles with the numbers 1-25 painted on the candles' circumferences. Beginning December 1, burn down through the numbers, day by day, until Christmas arrives. With the house all dark except for the candle's light, children love to watch the tiny flame. Each night when the next day's line is reached, the children can take turns blowing out the candle.

The candlelit time each evening is a good chance for quiet reflection on Christ who is the Light of the world.

*I am the light of the world:
he that followeth me shall not walk in darkness,
but shall have the light of life.*

JOHN 8:12

Advent Wake-Up Call

Early on the first day of Advent, gather a bunch of kids to go through the neighborhood singing Christmas carols. Leave a small Advent gift (a candle, a set of cards, baked goods) on the steps of each household.

The generous prosper and are satisfied.
PROVERBS 11:25 NLT

Advent Prayer Requests

Have children write personal prayer requests on 25 slips of paper and place them in a basket. Starting on December 1, every morning have each child remove a prayer request. He or she is then responsible to pray for that concern throughout the day. Make sure the children understand that prayer requests are confidential.

All things, whatsoever ye shall ask in prayer, believing, ye shall receive.
MATTHEW 21:22

Jesse Tree

This is a special tree that reminds children of the Old Testament stories that pointed to the coming of Christ. You may want to use a smaller Christmas tree for this, or even a large houseplant. Each ornament for the tree symbolizes an Old Testament story; for instance, a ladder represents Jacob; little tablets, the law of Moses; a rainbow, the story of Noah; a harp for David; a trumpet for the walls of Jericho; a sheaf of wheat for Ruth and Naomi; a scroll, Isaiah's prophecy, and so on. Use your knowledge of the Bible to come up with your own ornament ideas, and ask your children for their help. Each night of Advent, tell an Old Testament story and have a child hang on the Jesse tree the ornament that goes with that story. This will help children understand the connection between Christ's coming and the Old Testament.

*All the prophets from Samuel
and those that follow after,
as many as have spoken,
have likewise foretold of these days.*

ACTS 3:24

Advent Lullabies

When my children were small, during Advent I often tucked them in bed to the music of Christmas carols. You might even want to encourage your children to continue singing as they lie quietly in their beds. I always found this was a good way to help children relax—and a wonderful way to fight the nighttime fears to which children are sometimes prone.

Let the saints be joyful...
let them sing aloud upon their beds.
PSALM 149:5

Christmas Caroling

Don't forget this old-fashioned Advent activity. Be sure to sing at the homes of shut-ins who may be especially lonely this time of year. Children can learn the names of elderly church or community members whom they rarely see, and they can experience the joy and thankfulness these people feel. It can be a marvelous giving experience.

Speaking to yourselves in
psalms and hymns and spiritual songs,
singing and making melody in your heart to the Lord.
EPHESIANS 5:19

Advent Culture

When I was growing up, each year our family attended a local performance of *The Messiah*. Although I was very young when I first attended this very beautiful, but very long concert, I remember how excited and grown up I felt in my dressed-up clothes. My mother had helped me to learn Isaiah 9:6, and I was excited to hear the words I knew being sung. To this day, whenever I hear the strains of *The Messiah*, I have the same tingly sense of excitement and joy—and whenever I read that verse from Isaiah, I hear Handel's triumphant music.

Examples of other "Advent culture" children will enjoy are *The Nutcracker* ballet, the opera *Amahl and the Night Visitors*, or a dramatic performance of *A Christmas Carol*. Before the event, read the story out loud to familiarize children with the basic plots.

Don't assume your children are too young to appreciate the music and message of these wonderful Christmas cultural events.

> *For unto us a child is born, unto us a son is given:*
> *and the government shall be upon his shoulder:*
> *and his name shall be called Wonderful, Counsellor,*
> *The mighty God, The everlasting Father, The Prince of Peace.*
> ISAIAH 9:6

Person of the Week

If you have more than four children, divide the days of Advent by the number of children. Then focus on one individual during each week or group of days. Discuss that person's year—successes, disappointments, areas of growth, changes. Every day, pray for the person of the week. This is a good way to affirm a child's individuality and unique strengths.

You are each so important to the Kingdom!
Never forget that fact.
GWYNETH GAVIN

Advent Quilts

Why not spend some time during Advent sewing together as a family? Making quilted sleeping bags from old blankets and scraps of cloth is a way to share some warmth with those who have no home at Christmas. Or for a smaller project, sew a crib quilt for an AIDS baby.

This family activity is probably better for older children. My eleven-year-old has been sewing straight seams on the sewing machine for a couple of years now, and my nine-year-old and six-year-old can make the knots that hold the layers of cloth together. These quilts do not have to be works of art, merely warm and serviceable demonstrations of love.

He that hath mercy on the poor, happy is he.
PROVERBS 14:21

Messages of Love

A mother I know shares this Advent activity: "Each year our kids look around to see if they know someone who is in some kind of trouble—financial, physical, or emotional. Then we think how and what we can give anonymously that will be of practical help and bring encouragement as well. The secrecy is half the fun, but giving ourselves is the best part. This activity means even more during those times when money is a little short for our own family. Doing with less, so we can still have enough to give away, has been a true blessing. The children feel as though each year they get to help the angels bring God's message of love."

*But when you give to the needy,
do not let your left hand know
what your right hand is doing,
so that your giving may be in secret.
Then your Father,
who sees what is done in secret,
will reward you.*

MATTHEW 6:3–4 NIV

Advent Brainstorming

Most of us spend too much at Christmastime—but rather than announcing to your children that this year they're not going to get that bicycle or computer program they're hoping for, involve them in the process of cutting back as a family. Have a family meeting at the beginning of Advent and brainstorm ways your family can spend less this year at Christmas. Have a "secretary" make notes and take even the youngest children's ideas seriously. Vote on which ideas you will put into practice this year and then be accountable to one another throughout the holidays.

*The true spirit of Christmas is
not about spending—
it's about giving—
from the heart more than
from the pocketbook.*

ANONYMOUS

Advent Letters

If you send a Christmas letter with your cards, why not let your children have a part in creating it? Ask them to tell about their year's activities and achievements; encourage them to express some of their thoughts and feelings as well. Younger children can dictate their letters.

Not only will friends and relatives enjoy reading the kids' letters, but this is a good way for children to reflect on the past year and to see all that God has done for them.

O taste and see that the LORD is good.
PSALM 34:8

An Extra Place at the Table

At special Advent meals, set one extra place—for the Christ Child. This is a concrete reminder to children that Christ is always present with us.

Lo, I am with you alway.
MATTHEW 28:20

Family Pajama Party

Some time during Advent, on a night when no one has to be anywhere early the next morning, get out the sleeping bags and have a family pajama party. Eat popcorn and Christmas cookies (don't worry about the crumbs), read the Christmas story or have the children act it out, and sing Christmas carols. With the Christmas tree lights glowing in the darkness, stay up late talking about the things that really matter to you.

Some of my best Christmas memories are of the simplest little things....

GWYNETH GAVIN

Blessing Breakfast

On the first day of Advent, begin the Christmas season with a special time of family blessing. Get up a little earlier so you have time for a relaxed breakfast. (That's always a challenge in my house, but the rewards are worth the extra effort.) At the center of your table put a large white candle to symbolize Christ. Then place around it smaller candles for each member of the family. When all the children are assembled, light the center candle with a prayer of thanksgiving to Christ, and one by one light the other candles. (Older children can light their own.) As you light each candle, bless your children by saying, "You, [name], are a gift of God to us." When all the candles are lit, you might want to all say together, "We are all special to each other because of Jesus' love in us." Then enjoy your breakfast!

You are a gift of God.
You embody Jesus' love in our world.
No one else can shine in the same way you do.

LUCIE CHRISTOPHER

Get It on Tape

Throughout Advent keep a tape recorder handy, and from time to time have the kids tell about the day's happenings or reflect on the past year. On Christmas Day listen to the tape (or tapes) as a family. You might want to make copies to send to relatives who are far away. Next year at Christmas, listen to the tape again, to remind children of past memories and show them how they've grown.

"My goodness, how you've grown!"
my grandma would always say to me on Christmas Day.
I'd look down at myself—
and to my great surprise, I'd realize she was right!
GWYNETH GAVIN

Nativity Construction

This activity is good for a stormy afternoon in Advent. Give the kids newspapers, tape, and crayons, and ask them to create a life-size nativity scene. (If they draw around each other on taped-together newspapers they'll end up with life-size figures they can embellish with the crayons. They'll have to be more creative for the animals!) When Joseph, Mary, Jesus, the manger, wise men, shepherds, sheep, and cows are completed, tape them to a bare wall. Then calm the giggles by gathering around the manger and singing Christmas songs.

Joy to the World! The Lord is come.
ISAAC WATTS

Advent Sale

This is a good way to help younger children buy Christmas gifts and raise money for a charity at the same time. (It also gives children practice handling money.)

First ask an adult Sunday school class to donate small items (new or barely used) that children might enjoy giving as gifts to family members. Then ask a group of kids to bring their Christmas gift allowance to a Christmas sale. Involve them in the decision as to where to send the proceeds of this activity, so that they truly understand that their money is going to help others.

*Give to the poor,
and thou shalt have treasure in heaven.*

MARK 10:21

Interviewing the Older Generation

Ask children to interview older family members. (Or if you don't live close to family, take them for a visit to a nursing home.) They might want to ask questions like, "What was life like when you were my age?"; "When you were my age, what was your favorite thing to do?"; "Tell me about a time when God especially blessed you." Have them record the stories they hear in a notebook as a way of preserving their heritage. I've found this activity also helps create bridges of understanding between the generations. You might want to try it with a Sunday school class or youth group.

*Hear instruction, and be wise,
and refuse it not.*

Proverbs 8:33

Advent Treasure Hunt

Type up the Christmas story from the Gospel of Luke—and then cut it into strips, verse by verse. Hide the strips of paper around the house (or outdoors if weather permits). Then draw a treasure map, with a star to indicate where each piece of the story is. Once the children have found all the verses, have them put them in the correct order to read out loud. (Older children can do the reading for younger ones.) Conclude the activity with hot chocolate and Christmas cookies.

For unto you is born this day in the city of David a Saviour, which is Christ the Lord.
LUKE 2:11

A Time For History

This year make Advent a time for remembering the past as you reflect on Christ's coming. Visit historical sites and museums; talk about immigrant stories; do research to find how historical events affected ancestors. This is a great learning activity for older children, but it is also a way for them to see our heritage of blessing in Christ.

Yea, I have a goodly heritage.
PSALM 16:6

Family Portraits

Throughout Advent, have children work on drawings of themselves. You may want to do this on separate sheets of paper or on a single sheet for a family group. If you save these from year to year, they allow kids to look back at their growth. You may even want to frame them!

They are not our children, Lord. They are Yours. . . .
EMILIE GRIFFIN

Psalm Bag

This Advent meal tradition is said to come from Germany. In a cloth bag—in old days this would have been a salt sack—put small squares of cardboard with the numbers from 1-150. Before each meal, one child picks a number and then reads the appropriate psalm from the Bible.

Be filled with the Spirit;
Speaking to yourselves in psalms.
EPHESIANS 5:18–19

Advent Nativity

This activity involves collecting 24 nativity pieces—Mary, Joseph, shepherds, wise men, angels, sheep, donkeys—and as many other animals as you can find! Keep all the figures in a basket and on each day of Advent have children take turns adding another figure to a nativity scene that you have displayed in a central place. Some days you may want to read an appropriate passage of Scripture.

My children have decided that many of their small animal figures would enjoy being a part of Christmas, so this helps stretch the nativity figures. As they place each figure day by day, the story of Jesus' birth unfolds before their eyes.

*And she shall bring forth a son,
and thou shalt call his name JESUS:
for he shall save his people from their sins.*

MATTHEW 1:21

Soup Week

One family I know has a "soup week" for one week during Advent. Each evening they have a simple meal of soup and bread—and then they send the money they've saved on food as a gift to overseas relief. What a good way to help children share their hearts with a needy world!

*If you spend yourselves in behalf of the hungry
and satisfy the needs of the oppressed,
then your light will rise in the darkness,
and your night will become like the noonday.*

ISAIAH 58:10 NIV

Mitten Tree

As a Sunday school or youth activity, invite each member of the group to bring one or more pairs of new or nearly new mittens to hang on a tree throughout Advent. After Christmas, give the mittens to a homeless shelter to distribute. Make sure the children understand that because of their generosity, another child will have warm hands.

Give, and it shall be given unto you;
good measure, pressed down, and shaken together.
LUKE 6:38

A Jar Full of Blessings

Throughout the year, as God answers a prayer, have kids write it down on a slip of paper and put it into a jar. During Advent, let the children take turns reading all the blessings God has provided.

*The blessing of the LORD, it maketh rich,
and he addeth no sorrow with it.*
PROVERBS 10:22

Help a Charity

During the month of December, charities like the Salvation Army and food cupboards need all the help they can get. As a family or with a group of Sunday school kids, help sort the donated canned and boxed foods; pack food boxes and toy bags for needy families; be available for whatever chores need doing. Even young children can be useful with a little supervision.

*Do good. . .be rich in good deeds. . .
be generous and willing to share.*
1 TIMOTHY 6:18 NIV

Create a Family History Book

Buy an inexpensive blank book or scrapbook, and throughout Advent have children work on writing down the year's stories. Include drawings and photographs. You might want to also have a space for postcards, treasured greeting cards, or letters the children have received throughout the year from Grandma and Grandpa. This is a good way to "save memories," and children will enjoy reading through it again next Advent.

Write this for a memorial in a book.
EXODUS 17:14

Dipping Day

In their book, *Celebrate the Wonder, a Family Christmas Treasury,* Kristen Tucker and Rebecca Warren tell about a particularly harsh December that created a famine in Scandinavian countries. Many households had only thin broth and black bread available for the usually plentiful holiday suppers—but nevertheless they celebrated the Lord's coming by sharing their simple fare.

"Dipping Day," a family ceremony of sharing, is a Swedish tradition that commemorates that long-ago holiday season. Families stand around a pot of broth, and each person in turn dips a chunk of bread into the broth with a prayer for God's blessings in the coming year. To share this custom with a group of kids, prepare a pot of broth and place a loaf of unsliced bread nearby. Each child takes a turn at breaking off a chunk of bread and dipping it into the broth. Have each child share a prayer.

*Trust in the L*ORD*, and do good;*
so shalt thou dwell in the land,
and verily thou shalt be fed.
PSALM 37:3

Folk Traditions

This Advent, why not encourage your kids to explore their ethnic heritage? Many meaningful Advent folk traditions are being slowly swallowed up by more homogeneous, commercialized activities. Dozens of books in the public library can help kids in their research. . .or have them ask their oldest surviving family members for information on what traditions were observed when they were children. Then help your kids celebrate these ethnic traditions in your home this Advent.

*Christmas ties us to the past.
We celebrate the good years and the bad,
the long bleak eras that slowly but surely
brought us to today.*

ALEXANDER PHILLIPS

Advent Grocery Shopping

Take the children grocery shopping and fill up a sack with Christmas goodies—chocolate chips, nuts, butter, brown sugar—all the expensive ingredients you need for Christmas baking. Be sure to involve the children in selecting the items. Then go together to a food cupboard or shelter and leave the groceries to be given to a needy family.

Share with God's people who are in need.
ROMANS 12:13 NIV

Advent Dress Up

Shop at a thrift store for robes, scarves, jewelry, etc. that young children can use to playact the story of Jesus' birth.

And the Word was made flesh, and dwelt among us,
(and we beheld his glory,
the glory as of the only begotten of the Father,)
full of grace and truth.
JOHN 1:14

Global Advent

Help children become more aware of the other inhabitants of the world. To increase their understanding of the physical size of the planet, you might give them a globe, a poster of the earth as seen from outer space, or an atlas. *National Geographic* and mission magazines are a good way to get a visual idea of how other cultures live around the world. As your family Christmas shops, you might want to take advantage of the wonderful gifts available from UNICEF—or from a Christian organization like Ten Thousand Villages. The items these organizations offer are not only well-made and lovely, but your family's money will go to help children in developing nations.

*Charge them that are rich in this world,
that they be not highminded,
nor trust in uncertain riches,
but in the living God,
who giveth us richly all things to enjoy.*

1 TIMOTHY 6:17

A Hungry World

We live in a hungry world—and yet throughout Advent most of our own family meals will be rich and plentiful.

I think God wants us to enjoy and thank Him for the many blessings He has given us—but I am also certain He wants His people to share with those who have fewer material blessings, whether they are next door or across the world.

I delight in giving my children things at Christmastime, but I need to remind myself that one of the most important gifts I can give them is an awareness of the needs around them —and a willingness to share.

Here are some organizations that are concerned with world hunger that would appreciate your children's involvement at Advent (and all year long):

Bread for the World
6411 Chillum Place, N.W.
Washington, DC 20012

CROP
P.O. Box 968
Elkhart, IN 46514

Mennonite Central Committee
21 South 12th Street
Akron, PA 17501

Church World Service
475 Riverside Drive
New York, NY 10026

These books on world food needs are excellent resources for you and your kids:

Bread for the World by Arthur Simon (Eerdmans)

Diet for a Small Planet by Frances Moore Lappé (Ballantine)

Enough is Enough by John V. Taylor (Augsburg)

Food First by Frances M. Lappé and Joseph Collins (Ballantine)

More with Less Cookbook by Doris Janzen Longacre (Herald Press)

Rich Christians in an Age of Hunger by Ronald J. Sider (Inter-Varsity Press)

The Twenty-Ninth Day by Lester Brown (Norton)

Living More with Less by Doris Janzen Longacre (Herald Press)

Loaves and Fishes by Linda Hunt, Marianne Frase, and Doris Liebert (Herald Press)

Advent Peace

Since peace begins at home, during the month of December encourage your kids to play only games that require cooperation rather than competition.

And let the peace of God rule in your hearts.
COLOSSIANS 3:15

Family Calendar

For young children, make a picture calendar so they can count off the days till the special events of Advent. For example, draw a tree on the day you plan to get the tree, gingerbread men on the day you plan to bake cookies, airplanes on the day that Grandma and Grandpa are flying in, a Bible on Sundays, and a big birthday cake on Jesus' birthday. Young children will derive a sense of satisfaction from knowing when events will occur; this activity teaches young children calendar skills as well as heightens their anticipation and excitement.

Behold the day, behold, it is come.
EZEKIEL 7:10

Santa Claus—Or Not?

Are you uncomfortable with Santa Claus? My first Advent as a mother I made the decision that my children would not grow up believing in Santa Claus—but a few years later they decided on their own that Santa Claus was real, no matter what their skeptical mother might believe. Although I was sometimes uncomfortable with their belief, they seemed to grasp the spiritual essence of Santa Claus that I had missed.

Here's one author's solution to the Santa Claus dilemma from the December 1896 issue of *Good Housekeeping*:

Tell the child the dear old stories of the good Saint as often as you please, but tell them invariably as myths, as fairy tales. Tell them from babyhood, when the letter will be all he will understand, until he reaches the age when he can grasp the spiritual idea and slough the letter off. If the child is always told the myth of Santa Claus as a fairy tale, he will have all the childish joy and will have nothing to unlearn. You need not fear that he will lose the child's right to happiness in the story because of this way of presenting it. To a child of three, the spiritual is unintelligible and the tale will be a simple actuality; when he reaches the age of five or six, his mind will readjust it to an ideality. Tell the child the truth, by all means, but remember that for him, as for all children, some of the deepest truths lie in the realm of fairy tale.

Whatever choice you make in regards to Santa Claus, don't make the jolly old fellow more important than the Child he originally served.

Christ is the one true Light that burns
undimmed at the heart of Christmas.
Santa Claus, Christmas trees, family gatherings,
are all lesser planets that circle this one Star.
They shine with bright beauty
only when they reflect His light.
LUCIE CHRISTOPHER

Every Day Is Special

At the beginning of Advent sit down with your children and a calendar—and decide on an activity for each day to make that day a celebration. Examples might be "Kids Choose the Menu Day," "Hear a Story as Many Times as You Want Day," "Decorate the Tree Day," "Christmas Cookie Day," etc.

This is the day which the Lord hath made;
we will rejoice and be glad in it.
PSALM 118:24

Gingerbread People

On the first day of Advent bake 24 gingerbread people with your children. Allow yourself plenty of time. (I find that if I try to squeeze an activity like this into a busy day, I end up feeling pressured and grouchy—and when I'm feeling like that, it's not much fun for anyone involved!) Encourage your children to roll, cut, and decorate.

String the gingerbread people on a red ribbon for a Christmas garland in your kitchen. Have the children take turns each day selecting one gingerbread person to gobble. A great way to make concrete the countdown of days until Christmas!

Let us now go even unto Bethlehem, and see this thing which is come to pass, which the Lord hath made known unto us.
LUKE 2:15

Recipe for
Gingerbread Modeling Dough
(edible)

¾ cup margarine
1½ cups brown sugar
1½ cups molasses
10½ cups flour
¾ tsp soda

1½ tsp cloves
1½ tsp cinnamon
3 tsp ginger
1½ tsp salt
1 cup water

This dough will be very stiff. (Use your hands to mix.) Shape the gingerbread people the way you would if you were playing with Play-Doh. Use toothpicks to make holes in the heads for stringing on a ribbon. Bake at 350 degrees for 10-12 minutes, depending on thickness. Makes twenty-four 5-inch-long fat gingerbread people.

Taffy Pull

Reenact a pioneer Christmas tradition. Invite a dozen children to participate in a taffy pull. One child can mix the ingredients. An older child can monitor the candy thermometer. Two kids can cut the paper to wrap the candies. Younger children can butter the cooking trays. Everyone will want turns pulling the taffy, and when the taffy is done, everyone can sit around a table to shape and wrap the candy.

I bring you good tidings of great joy,
which shall be to all people.
LUKE 2:10

Recipe for Taffy

1 cup sugar
¾ cup light corn syrup
⅔ cup water
1 tbsp cornstarch

2 tbsp butter or
   margarine
1 tsp salt
2 tsp vanilla

In a 2-quart saucepan, combine all ingredients except vanilla. Cook over medium heat, stirring constantly, to 256 degrees on a candy thermometer (or until a small amount of the mixture dropped into cold water forms a hard ball). Remove from heat and stir in vanilla. Pour into an 8 x 8 x 2-inch square pan.

When taffy is just cool enough to handle, pull it with buttered fingers until it is light in color and stiff and satiny. Pull into long strips, ½ inch wide, then cut with scissors into 1-inch pieces. Wrap pieces individually in plastic wrap or waxed paper. Makes about a pound.

Family Museum

Throughout Advent, ask your kids to assemble items for a "Family Museum." They may want to include favorite toys, schoolwork, photographs, or family heirlooms. Display your museum in a central place. This activity builds family togetherness and identity.

And of his fulness have all we received, and grace for grace.
JOHN 1:16

Advent Games

Make Advent a time of old-fashioned family games. One favorite from my own childhood is Hide the Thimble, where a thimble (or button or other small object) is hidden somewhere in the room by one person, and sought by the others until it is found. Children of all ages can participate in this game.

Other choices might be Blind Man's Bluff or Simon Says. You'd be surprised how much fun games like these can be (even for adults).

Thou shalt rejoice, thou, and thine household.
DEUTERONOMY 14:26

Christmas Pantomime

On slips of paper write down activities that can be mimed. For instance:

- buying a Christmas present
- trimming a Christmas tree
- wrapping a large package with a small piece of paper
- selecting a Christmas tree

Or you may want to write down activities from the biblical narrative of the nativity, such as:

- Joseph and Mary on their way to Bethlehem

- the shepherds running to see the Baby
- the wise men following the star
- the innkeeper turning away Joseph and Mary

Then have the kids take turns pulling a slip of paper and acting out the activity, while the others try to guess what he or she is doing.

Away in the manger, no crib for a bed,
The little Lord Jesus laid down His sweet head.
ANONYMOUS

Carol Relays

One fun way to break the ice with a gathering of kids during Advent is to sing Christmas carols in relays. One member of the circle starts the carol by singing just one line, the next person sings the second line, and so on until the song is finished.

Joy to the earth! The Savior reigns;
Let men their songs employ.
ISAAC WATTS

Advent Animals

Here's another Advent game to play with kids. Write the names of animals of the Bible on cards, with two cards for each animal. Then pass the cards out to a group of children. (You'll need an even number of kids.) After the cards have been distributed, one lamb must hunt through the crowd for the other lamb, one lion for the other lion, etc. When the animals have been paired, each couple looks up a Bible verse that mentions their particular animal and reads it out loud to the group. This also makes a great ice breaker.

We'll keep our Christmas merry still.
SIR WALTER SCOTT

Advent Word Game

Distribute pencils and paper to each child and ask them to make as many words as they can from the letters in the words "ADVENT MEANS THE COMING OF CHRIST." This is a good game for the car on long holiday trips.

May the grace of Christ our Savior
And the Father's boundless love,
With the Holy Spirit's favor,
Rest upon us from above.
JOHN NEWTON

Christmas Scents

This is another holiday game that the whole family can play—and it doesn't require an expensive board game. After supper, for a time of laughter and fun, present the family with a tray containing small paper bags of various things with a distinct aroma. Pass the tray around so that every child can take a sniff, testing his or her olfactory nerves. See if they can identify the items correctly.

Suggested articles:

pine needles	cedar shavings	coffee
tea	cheese	piece of apple
orange	peppermint candy	spices
onion	olives	tuna fish

*All thy works shall praise thee,
O Lord;
and thy saints shall bless thee.*

Psalm 145:10

Spelling Bee

This is yet another old-fashioned way for children to amuse themselves. During Advent take turns spelling different Christmas words (like star, shepherd, manger, etc.—depending on each child's learning level). This activity can be done anytime—around the dinner table, in the car, waiting in the dentist's office, or standing in line at the grocery store.

Both young men, and maidens;
old men, and children:
Let them praise the name of the LORD.
PSALM 148:12–13

Another Old-Fashioned Game

Begin by saying to a group of kids, "You are each a wise man bringing gifts to the Christ Child." Then each child in turn must think of a gift for each letter of the alphabet. For instance, "I will give Him amber," "I will give Him blessings," "I will give Him a carnation," etc. Some of the answers may be quite hilarious. If someone gets stuck, allow him or her to ask for help from the others.

What can I give Him,
Poor as I am?
If I were a shepherd
I would bring a lamb;
If I were a wise man
I would do my part;
yet what can I give Him—
Give Him my heart.

CHRISTINA ROSSETTI

Art in the Dark

Distribute pencils and paper to all the children. Then turn out the lights and ask each person to draw a picture to illustrate a scene from the Nativity story. When the lights are turned on, see if the others can guess what each has drawn in the dark.

The light shineth in the darkness;
and the darkness comprehended it not.
JOHN 1:5

Musical Wreath

The only material needed for this variation of musical chairs is a large wreath. Have the tallest child in your family or Sunday school class hold this wreath high above the heads of the children as they pass under it, while Christmas carols are played on a tape. When the music stops, the child drops the wreath over whoever happens to be directly under it. The captured child is eliminated from the procession. This continues until the last child is caught.

Let the children of Zion be joyful in their King.
PSALM 149:2

Unwrapping the Present

Here's yet another simple variation on musical chairs. Place an inexpensive gift in a small box. Wrap paper around the package until you have a dozen or more wrappings, each securely and separately fastened. With the players in a circle, begin passing the package around as Christmas music plays. While the music plays, the package is passed from hand to hand, but as soon as the music stops, the player holding the package starts to unwrap it. The break in the music should be frequent but only for a few seconds at a time. When the music starts again, the package is again passed along. This is continued until the package is finally unwrapped. The player who uncovers the present is allowed to keep it. Or better yet, fill the box with small objects like stickers or candy, enough to share with everyone.

Cheerfully share.

1 PETER 4:9 NLT

Trimming the Tree

This activity takes the hassle out of decorating the tree. After you set up your Christmas tree, leave it bare except for the lights. Place the ornaments in a box beside the tree. Then each time a child does an act that expresses the true spirit of Christmas, he or she gets to hang a decoration on the tree. (Obviously, the decorations will need to be "child friendly.")

Your tree may not end up looking like Martha Stewart decorated it. But it will be a testament to your children's love and goodwill for one another.

O Christmas tree, O Christmas tree,
How lovely are your branches.

GERMAN CAROL

The Giving Tree

Have a small second Christmas tree in your house where throughout Advent children can place gifts for the needy. (Or you could do this activity at church for Sunday school classes or youth groups.) They might want to use their own spending money to buy gifts, or they can wrap nearly new toys that they would like to share with someone who has less than them. At the end of Advent, go together as a group to deliver the gifts to a local shelter or other charity.

*Each man should give what
he has decided in his heart to give,
not reluctantly or under compulsion,
for God loves a cheerful giver.*

2 CORINTHIANS 9:7 NIV

Advent Pledge

At the beginning of Advent, give older children a chance to sign this pledge:

THIS ADVENT I COMMIT MYSELF. . .

- *to remember those people who truly need my gifts.*
- *to express my love for family and friends in more direct ways.*
- *to look for chances to share what I have—whether time, talent, or concrete objects—with those who have less than I.*
- *to examine each of my holiday activities in light of the true spirit of Christmas.*

- *to initiate acts of peacemaking within my circle of family and friends.*
- *to try to keep Christ at the center of each day as I prepare my heart to welcome His coming.*

For younger children, you might want to simplify the wording of this pledge and choose to include only one or two items. For very young kids, pick one thing to do each day, rather than asking them to make promises for the next four weeks.

*As many as received him,
to them gave he power to become the sons of God,
even to them that believe on his name.*
JOHN 1:12

Alternative Gift Days

While the rest of the world frantically counts down the shopping days, make a choice to voluntarily step out of the hectic whirl. Exchange gifts on another day (for instance, the first weekend of Advent or St. Nicholas Day—December 6—or after Christmas on Epiphany—January 6) rather than on Christmas Eve or Christmas Day. This allows you as a family to celebrate Advent simply as a time of spiritual meaning.

This activity needs to be agreed upon by the whole family, not just the parents, particularly if you have older children—so parents may need to do some patient lobbying with the kids.

*Let this mind be in you,
which was also in Christ Jesus.*

PHILIPPIANS 2:5

A Family Time Capsule

Advent is a time when memories are made. Capture those memories by creating a family time capsule to be opened in not less than five years. It need not be buried any deeper than the basement, garage, attic—or in my household, the back of the overflowing hall closet would work! Have kids collect items such as newspapers, photographs, drawings, homework assignments, etc., and place them in a mailing tube. Each child may want to include a wish or a dream for the years to come. Other items to include might be a video or audio tape of family members, a piece of jewelry to be given to a child when the capsule is opened, or fashion accessories to demonstrate the changeability of certain fads.

*Jesus Christ the same yesterday,
and to day, and for ever.*

HEBREWS 13:8

Kindness Box

During Advent, wrap up a shoebox like a present and cut a slot in the top. Then put the box and a pencil and a notepad under the tree. When someone in the family notices someone else being kind, write the act down on a piece of paper and put it in the box. (Young children could draw a picture—or tell Mom what they saw and ask her to write it down.) On Christmas Eve, open the box and read all the notes.

This is a twist on some of the other activities already mentioned (like "Making the Baby's Bed" and "Trimming the Tree"), because this time the emphasis is on noticing the kindness of others. We all take each other for granted sometimes; children (and adults!) learn from paying attention to often unnoticed small acts of daily kindness.

Be ye kind one to another.

EPHESIANS 4:32

Posada

This Mexican and Central American tradition is an activity that involves kids in the true meaning of Christmas. Each member of the family acts out the story of Mary and Joseph's search for somewhere to stay in Bethlehem. (*Posada* means "inn.") Go from room to room in your house, looking for somewhere that will welcome the Christ Child. Conclude the activity with a prayer that Christ will be welcome in each of your hearts.

Come and worship, come and worship,
Worship Christ, the newborn King!
JAMES MONTGOMERY

Secret Angels

This year have the children all choose "secret friends," individuals they promise to help in some way throughout Advent. These people might be younger brothers or sisters, a parent, a grandparent, an elderly neighbor. Then each "angel" thinks of ways to be of help without revealing their identity. (Younger children may need a parent's occasional help with this Advent activity.)

*When you give a gift to someone in need,
don't shout about it.*
MATTHEW 6:2 NLT

Fathers-and-Children Day

One Saturday during Advent, send Father and children off to the mall for a day of fun and Christmas shopping. This gives them precious time together—and gives Mother a day off. Make this activity a tradition each year!

The glory of children are their fathers.
PROVERBS 17:6

Take the Pledge!

Pledge to reduce your children's television viewing during the holiday season and replace those hours with family activities such as the ones described in this book.

Be renewed in the spirit of your mind.
EPHESIANS 4:23

Nature Hike

Make a nature hike one of your Advent traditions. A snowy walk in the woods is a wonderful opportunity for family closeness—and it's also a chance to collect greenery and pinecones for decorating your home.

*Mountains and all hills; fruitful trees, and all cedars. . .
Let them praise the name of the LORD:
for his name alone is excellent.*
PSALM 148:9, 13

Snow Fun

As a family, build a giant snow castle, shape a family of snow people (one for each member of the family), or construct an igloo fort for a snowball battle. This activity is even better if Mom and Dad participate too!

Hast thou entered into the treasures of the snow?
JOB 38:22

Advent for the Birds

At the beginning of December have the kids string popcorn and cranberries for a "bird's Christmas tree." They can also decorate the tree with pinecones covered with cheap peanut butter and then rolled in birdseed. This activity reminds children that God's love and care extends even to the natural world around us.

Beasts, and. . .flying fowl. . .
*Let them praise the name of the L*ORD.
PSALM 148:10, 13

Happy Faces

With red and green markers, make a banner to hang over your door that reads: MAKE SOMEONE HAPPY TODAY! If you include a row of smiley faces, this reminder will work with even the youngest children. It's a simple way to spread the joy of Christ all through the season.

The joy of the LORD is your strength.
NEHEMIAH 8:10

Visiting the Lonely

Since Christmas is an especially lonely time for nursing home residents, make it an Advent tradition to visit them each year.

When we first did this, my youngest daughter was startled, if not a bit frightened, by the wistful hands that reached out to touch her hair and cheeks as she walked down the corridor. Since then, however, she's come to understand that even a glimpse of a child's bright face makes the day special for people who feel forlorn and discouraged—and a child's hug and kiss is better than any other gift!

Continue to love each other with true Christian love.

HEBREWS 13:1 NLT

Plum Pudding

As a family, make a plum pudding the Saturday after Thanksgiving. The kids can help with the chopping and mixing. After it's done, store it in plastic wrap and refrigerate. It takes about a month to become softer, darker, and more flavorful. (And it tastes better, in my opinion, than fruitcake.) Anticipation. . . !

Recipe for Plum Pudding

2²⁄₃ cups dark raisins
2 cups dried currants

2 cups water

Cover and simmer for 20 minutes, then remove cover, and cook, stirring occasionally, until most of liquid has evaporated. Let cool to room temperature.

Combine in a bowl:

1½ cups flour
8 oz ground or finely
   chopped beef suet
1 cup firmly packed
   dark brown sugar

1½ tsp cinnamon
1½ tsp ginger
½ tsp cloves
½ tsp salt

In a separate bowl, mix together:

4 large eggs 2 tsp vanilla
½ cup rum flavoring

Add to flour mixture, along with the cooked raisin mixture. If you want, you can also add:

½ cup finely chopped dates
¼ cup finely chopped citron

Pour the batter into a greased 3-quart casserole and cover with a lid or aluminum foil. Put a rack or a folded dishtowel at the bottom of a pot that is large enough to accommodate the casserole dish. Set the casserole inside the pot, and pour enough boiling water into the pot to come two-thirds of the way up the sides of the casserole dish. Cover the pot tightly, and bring it to a boil over high heat; then lower the heat to maintain a high simmer. Replenish the water as necessary, and steam the pudding for 3½ hours. When done, the pudding should be firm in the center and dark around the edges. Using oven mitts, remove the pudding from the pot and cool to room temperature before inverting to free the pudding from the casserole dish. Store for up to 1 month.

To reheat, put the pudding back in the original dish and steam again for 1½-2 hours.

The Gift of Baby-Sitting

If you have older children, encourage them to offer their services as baby-sitters to relieve parents at this busy time of the year. Their gift will be especially meaningful to families who would not otherwise be able to afford a sitter.

And all thy children shall be taught of the LORD;
and great shall be the peace of thy children.
ISAIAH 54:13

Spreading Cheer

Help your children pack and decorate baskets of Christmas treats for hospital patients. You might want to include things like magazines, scented lotions, books of crossword puzzles, etc. Then get permission from a local hospital to deliver the baskets as a family. The hospital staff may be able to point you to those patients who are most in need of a little Advent cheer.

I exhort you to be of good cheer.
ACTS 27:22

Greeting Cards

This year involve the kids in at least one item on your to-do list: Have them help you send out Christmas cards. You might want them to simply write a short note and sign the family's name—or they can become involved at an even deeper level and actually create the cards.

Some years I've had my children make cards from construction paper, glue, and pictures cut from catalogs, magazines, and old Christmas cards. Other years they've drawn their own pictures for special cards, while I've duplicated their drawings for the rest. Now they're getting old enough to design their own cards on the computer. Not only does this save me time—it saves money as well.

Greet ye one another. . . .
The grace of our Lord Jesus Christ be with you.

1 Corinthians 16:20, 23

Advent Drives

This activity is simple and costs nothing: Simply bundle up the kids, and go out for a drive to see the Christmas lights in your neighborhood. You might want to sing carols as you go.

Oh the lights of Christmas!
How they glow in my memories of childhood!
ARCHER THALASSA

Forced Flowers

Bring branches of flowering trees (like forsythia or redbud) into the indoor warmth to make them bloom early. If you bring the branches inside on December 4, and stand them in water in a warm room, you should have blossoms by Christmas. As children watch the growing blooms throughout the Advent season, help them make the connection to Christ, who gives new life to us all, even in the midst of the coldest winters.

I will give thee a crown of life.
REVELATIONS 2:10

A Supper of Stars

Some evening during Advent, have a special "star supper." Try to make and arrange as many foods as you can into star shapes. Use star-shaped ice cubes colored with red and green food coloring; have star cookies for dessert; sprinkle silver star confetti across the tablecloth. After supper read the story of the wise men and the star to your young ones.

*Where is he that is born King of the Jews?
for we have seen his star in the east,
and are come to worship him.*
MATTHEW 2:2

Advent Mail

Young children love getting mail. This year why not mail your children notes of love, silly cards, and small gifts several times throughout the holiday season? Even if you don't have the time or energy for any other activity, you can almost always manage to drop a note into the mail. And somehow the fact that it came through the mail makes your message more "official."

I will pour out my Spirit on your offspring,
and my blessings on your descendants.
ISAIAH 44:3 NIV

A Little at a Time

Instead of decorating your house all at once (a huge task that generally falls on the mother's shoulders), this year make decorating a part of your Advent activities. Each day, starting with the first day of Advent, one child puts up another decoration. You'll have to wait for the full effect, but sometimes anticipation is half the fun. Remember, children often enjoy the process more than any perfect end result.

*I will praise thee, O LORD,
with my whole heart;
I will shew forth all thy marvellous works.*

PSALM 9:1

Christmas Cookies

No Advent would be complete without a day of old-fashioned, rolled-out cookie creation. If you're pressed for time, go ahead and cheat: Buy the rolls of pre-made dough you'll usually find near the dairy section in your grocery store. The fun part for the kids is rolling and cutting—like Play-Doh you get to eat! Get as many colors of frosting and decorator sugars as you can, and allow children to spread and sprinkle to their hearts' content. These cookies aren't intended for any *Good Housekeeping* competition—they're simply meant to provide times of family fun and sweetness.

My son, eat thou honey, because it is good.

PROVERBS 24:13

A Manger Instead of a Tree

Instead of having a Christmas tree be the focus of your holiday decorations this year, consider using a manger instead. You can use a large doll in a box or a cradle; if you like, use evergreen branches instead of straw. You might even want to create a bower of evergreen branches and Christmas lights to shelter the manger. Then put your gifts around the manger as you would a tree. This helps even the youngest child understand that Jesus is the real center of Christmas.

*The stars in the bright sky
looked down where He lay,
The little Lord Jesus asleep in the hay.*

ANONYMOUS

Carols from Other Lands

This year try learning Christmas carols from other countries and singing them together as a family as a part of your Advent celebrations. (You can find tapes or CDs in a music store, and the public library will have books of traditional Christmas music.) Use these songs to remind kids that Jesus came not only for our country, but for the entire world.

*Everywhere, everywhere,
Christmas tonight!
For the Christ-Child who comes
is the Master of all.*

PHILLIPS BROOKS

Relax!

This is one of the most important Advent traditions of all—but it's not an activity. Instead, it's just the reverse.

As much fun as Advent can be, it can also be a busy and stressful time of year, for kids as well as adults. If you schedule too much during these weeks, activities will begin to feel more like work and less like fun. Make it a family tradition to set aside time during the holiday season that's not scheduled in any way, time when kids and adults can simply *be*.

*There remains, then,
a Sabbath-rest for the people of God. . . .
Let us, therefore,
make every effort to enter that rest.*

HEBREWS 4:9, 11 NIV

Spreading Light

Throughout Advent, keep lighted candles in your windows. (Electric candles are less of a fire hazard.) This old German custom was originally meant to welcome passersby, assuring them of welcome and warmth if they were in need. It's a good reminder to kids that God calls us to open our hearts and our homes to anyone who might need our help.

*I was a stranger, and ye took me in....
Inasmuch as ye have done it unto one of
the least of these my brethren,
ye have done it unto me.*

MATTHEW 25:35, 40

Advent Puzzle

This is a quiet and stress-free Advent activity: Keep a jigsaw puzzle set up on a card table throughout the holiday season. Kids can work on it as they please.

Holidays should not be all excitement and fireworks.
We also need quiet times, peaceful times. . . .
ALEXIS WINTERS

Advent Guests

To teach kids to honor hospitality, make it a family practice to invite guests for meals during the Advent season. Ideally, these should not be simply friends and family, but also people who are outside your usual circle. Encourage the kids to suggest guest lists—and consider even the most unlikely suggestions.

Be not forgetful to entertain strangers:
for thereby some have entertained angels unawares.
HEBREWS 13:2

Sledding

If you have snow in your part of the country during the Advent season, make it a family tradition to spend at least one Saturday going sledding. Don't forget the hot chocolate afterward!

He spreads the snow like wool.
PSALM 147:16 NIV

Church Services

Most congregations offer several services throughout December that focus on the real meaning of Christmas. Don't get so busy scheduling other activities that you fail to leave your kids time for quiet worship in God's house.

*I was glad when they said unto me,
Let us go into the house of the LORD.*
PSALM 122:1

Their Very Own Trees

When my children were smaller, they liked to redecorate the tree every day. Here's an idea that avoids adult frustration and allows children to redecorate to their hearts' content.

Cut small branches from shrubbery or use branches trimmed off of your Christmas tree. Place the branches in a large can filled with gravel. Then give the children an assortment of unbreakable decorations and place each child's "tree" in his or her bedroom. As they grow older, you can let them put lights on the branches as well. They'll spend a lot of time in their rooms simply watching their "trees."

*As a child,
by the light of the Christmas tree
I saw wonders and magic,
elves and wood sprites.
But beyond that make-believe world,
I saw a Baby,
a real live Baby.*

LUCIE CHRISTOPHER

Advent Bake-athons

Set aside "baking days" throughout the Advent season when the whole family works together on holiday goodies. Even very young children can help stir, and older children can bake cookies all by themselves. Then package your goodies in decorated boxes and other containers, and deliver them as a family to neighbors and friends.

*Each one should use whatever gift
he has received to serve others.*
1 PETER 4:10 NIV

An After-Advent Activity

To make taking down the tree a little less painful, wrap a set of extra gifts in gold paper and put them deep under the tree for your kids, to be opened only after all the dismantling is complete. These "gifts of gold" are traditionally from the three wise men who presented their gifts to the Christ Child on Epiphany.

Behold, there came wise men from the east to Jerusalem. . . .
MATTHEW 2:1

A Ceremony For After Advent

As the holiday season draws to a close, gather the kids together to take the ornaments off the tree and carefully pack them away. If you have a cut tree, you might want to decorate it with food for the birds. Once your house is back to normal, have a time of quiet prayer, reminding children that Christ comes to us every day, not just at Advent. Discuss ways you can keep the Christmas spirit alive all year long.

*Rejoice! Rejoice!
Emmanuel
Shall come to thee,
O Israel.*

LATIN HYMN

Lord, may each of our activities be pleasing to You this Advent season. Each day, help us to prepare our hearts and lives and homes for Your coming.

Amen.